S0-DUS-027

MOSES AND THE GREAT ESCAPE

First published by Moody Press
c/o MLM,
Chicago, Illinois 60610,
U.S.A.

ISBN 0 8024 8487 5

Created and produced by Three's
Company, 12 Flitcroft Street,
London WC2H 8DJ

Worldwide co-edition organized and
produced by Angus Hudson Ltd

Design: Peter M. Wyart
Illustration research: Christine
Deverell
Typesetting by Watermark

Moses and the Great Escape

Stories retold by Tim Dowley; illustrations by Richard Deverell

Contents

Pharaoh's Slaves
The Day of the Frogs
Midnight Journey
The Desert Camp
The Golden Calf
Crossing Jordan

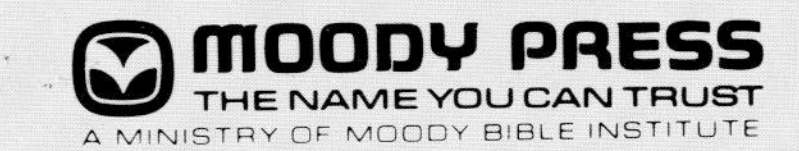

Pharaoh's Slaves

Pharaoh, the ruler of Egypt, watched from his great palace. He saw his Hebrew slaves working on the great buildings that were slowly risi[illegible]n the desert sands.

[illegible]r me!' he thought. 'All these[illegible]s are working for me, build[illegible]g me a new city. When it's finished, there will truly be something for the world to remember me by.'

But he was a worried king: 'When the Hebrew people first came to my land, more than four hundred years ago, there were only a few of them. But now look how many there are! Can I trust them? Won't they rise up against me?'

So Pharaoh made an order to his slave bosses:
'Crush the Hebrew slaves. Make them work even harder!'

But there also lived in Egypt a young man called Moses. Although he was the child of a Hebrew woman, he had been brought up in Pharaoh's palace by a royal princess.

One day Moses went out to watch the Hebrew slaves at work. Suddenly he saw an Egyptian cruelly beating a Hebrew slave. He was very angry to see one of his own people being so ill-treated. Moses looked about him, but he could see no one watching. So he killed the Egyptian and hid his body in the sand.

But soon afterwards Pharaoh came to hear that Moses had killed the Egyptian. He had to flee Egypt and go into hiding in another country.

Can you find?

You can find this story in the book of Exodus chapters 1 and 2.

Now look at the picture

Point to Pharaoh in his chariot.
How many Egyptian soldiers can you find?
What are the slaves doing on top of the arch?
Can you find a white bird flying past?
Where are the drawings of the palace?
Point to the slaves pulling a big stone up a slope.
What tools are the Hebrew slaves using?

Something to do

Now draw your own picture of the Hebrew slaves building Pharaoh's palace.

The Day of the Frogs

Many years later, two Hebrews came to Pharaoh in his palace. It was Moses and his brother, Aaron.

'What do you want?' asked Pharaoh proudly.

'The Lord our God has sent us. He says: "Let my people go! Let them go into the desert to worship me!"'

But Pharaoh laughed at them:

'Who is your God? And why should I take any notice of him?'

'If you don't do as God says, there will be illness and death in your land,' Moses replied.

Pharaoh simply grew angry:

'I won't let you stop my Hebrew slaves working. Just go away, and let my slaves alone.'

But after this, terrible things started to happen in Egypt. Moses' brother Aaron stretched out his rod over the river, and the water turned to blood. All the fish died, and the land was filled with an awful smell. The people were very worried because they couldn't find any water to drink.

But Pharaoh still refused to let the Hebrews go. So Aaron stretched out his rod again, and thousands and thousands of frogs hopped out of the water. They hopped everywhere – into people's houses, into Pharaoh's palace, into people's beds, and even into the pots and pans in the kitchens. 'Coark! Coark! Coark!' they croaked. The Egyptians were at their wits' end not knowing what to do. Then Moses and Aaron came to Pharaoh again:

'The Lord God says: "Let my people go!"'

But Pharaoh still refused to let the Hebrews leave Egypt.

Can you find?

You can find this story in Exodus chapters 7 and 8.

Now look at the picture

How many cats can you count?
Point to Moses and Aaron.
What do you think Pharaoh is saying?
Can you find any men with frogs on their heads?
What are the men putting into cooking pots?

Something to do

Draw a picture of Pharaoh eating his dinner, with frogs hopping everywhere.

Midnight Journey

After this many other terrible things happened in Egypt, but still Pharaoh would not let Moses take the Hebrew people out of his land. One day Moses had a new message for the Hebrews:

'Tonight we will have a special feast. Death is walking the land. But if you kill a lamb and smear its blood on the doorposts of your house, the Lord will pass by, and no one will be harmed. We will call this feast Passover, because death will pass over our homes.

'Then you must cook the lamb and some vegetables, and prepare dough to make bread. But don't put any yeast in the dough, so that the bread will stay flat when it's cooked.'

The people did just as Moses told them. But when they were ready to eat, a messenger came to Moses from Pharaoh:

'Pharaoh says "Go!" You must take everything with you and leave Egypt at once. Leave nothing behind!'

So the Hebrew families ate their special feast with all their outdoor clothes on. Then they left their homes in Egypt in the middle of the night, following their leader, Moses. They carried with them the unrisen dough. There was no time to cook it before they left. They would have to bake bread on their journey.

Pharaoh had told the Hebrews to take everything with them – their cattle, their furniture, their pots and pans, their clothes – and they did as he ordered. They even asked their Egyptian neighbours to give them silver and gold and jewels, and took these with them too.

And so the Hebrews set out on their long journey from Egypt, the land where they had been slaves, to their own land, the Promised Land.

Can you find?

You can find this story in Exodus 11–12.

Now look at the picture

Can you find Egyptians giving away their jewels?
Find someone who is still asleep.
Can you find someone kneading dough?
Can you find a cat in the picture?

Do you know which people still have a Passover meal every year?

The Desert Camp

After they had escaped from Pharaoh and his army, and safely crossed the Red Sea, Moses and the Hebrew people came to the desert. At night God led them in a pillar of fire, and by day in a pillar of cloud. He was with them all the time.

The Hebrews had escaped from being slaves in Egypt. God had set them free. Now they were making for their own country – Canaan, the Promised Land. They were learning to be God's people.

But there were many difficulties to face on the way. The Hebrews had to travel through the hot, dusty desert. They had to learn to live in tents. The Hebrews had been made to work very hard in Egypt, but at least they had had enough to eat. In the desert they sometimes didn't know where their next meal was coming from.

'Why did you bring us here to die?' they complained to Moses. 'We're starving. Our throats are parched. We'll die here. Why didn't we stay in Egypt? At least we had three good meals a day there!'

Moses listened patiently to their complaints, then answered: 'It's God you're complaining to. He brought you here. But he will save you. He'll look after you – even in the desert.'

And sure enough, that night a flock of birds called quails dropped exhausted near their camp. The Hebrews were amazed. They ran out and picked up the birds. Then they cooked and ate them, and thanked God for this unexpected feast.

Can you find?

You can find this story in Exodus chapter 16.

Now look at the picture of the desert camp

Can you find the pillar of cloud?
Point to a camel.
Can you find quails on a stick?
How many cows can you find?
Find a goat being milked.
What other animals can you see?
Where are the shields and spears?
Point to a campfire.

Something to do

Draw the Israelites on the march to their next campsite.

The Golden Calf

The Hebrew people went on marching day after day. After travelling many miles through the flat desert, they came to a land of high mountains. They were amazed to see such peaks towering into the sky. The people were a little frightened, especially when there was thunder and lightning as well.

God spoke to his people from the mountain and told Moses:

'Come up the mountain. I will speak to you there and give you my special laws for my people.'

So Moses climbed the mountain. He spent many days up on the mountain. At first the Hebrews waited patiently, but after a time they began to get frightened:

'Perhaps something terrible has happened to our leader, Moses. Perhaps he will never come back from the mountain...'

So they said to Aaron, Moses' brother:

'Make us a god we can see, and who will look after us.'

Aaron was afraid they might harm him if he didn't do as they asked. 'Bring me your gold earrings,' he said, 'and I will make a god for you.'

He melted down their earrings and made a golden calf out of them, like the idols the Egyptians worshipped.

At last Moses came down the mountain with his friend Joshua. He heard the Hebrews shouting and dancing in their camp.

'The people have forgotten God's commandment,' he said. 'God told us not to worship idols we have made.' Moses was so angry that he threw down the pieces of stone with God's laws written on them. Crash! They shattered into little pieces.

Can you find?

You can find this story in Exodus chapters 19, 20, and 32.

Now look at the picture

Point to the Hebrews dancing.
Can you find a man with a tambourine?
Find the stone that Moses has thrown down the mountain.
Where is the golden calf?

Something to do

Find out how many laws or rules were written on the pieces of stone. What were they called?

Crossing Jordan

Moses was still very angry when he reached the Hebrews' camp. He broke the golden calf into pieces and threw them into the fire. Then he went back up the mountain.

'The people are very sorry for what they have done. Will you forgive them?'

And God said: 'They are my people; I am their God.' He gave Moses two new stones with the laws written on them, and Moses returned to the Hebrews' camp.

But the Hebrews spent many more years wandering in the desert. They built a special big tent to show that God was living with them. They packed it up and carried it with them every time they moved camp. And there were many battles to fight and win before the Hebrews finally came to the river Jordan.

By now Moses was a very old man, and he knew he would not enter the Promised Land with his people. He had one last job to do. Moses called together the people and told them that Joshua would be their new leader. Then he left the camp and climbed a nearby mountain. The people never saw him again.

The Hebrews were finally ready to march into the Promised Land. But when they reached the banks of the river Jordan they found it was much too deep and much too fast-flowing for them to cross.

After three days, Joshua told the priests to cross the river with the ark of the covenant. This time the water dried up, and they marched across the dry river bed. And so all the Hebrew people crossed the river Jordan into the Promised Land. At last they had arrived in the land God had promised them.

Can you find?

You can find this story in Joshua chapters 3 and 4.

Now look at the picture

Find the mountain that Moses climbed.
What animals can you find?
How far does the line of Hebrews stretch?
Why are soldiers first across the river?

Something to do

Draw a picture of Moses leaving the camp for the last time.

How the Hebrews travelled from Egypt to the Promised Land

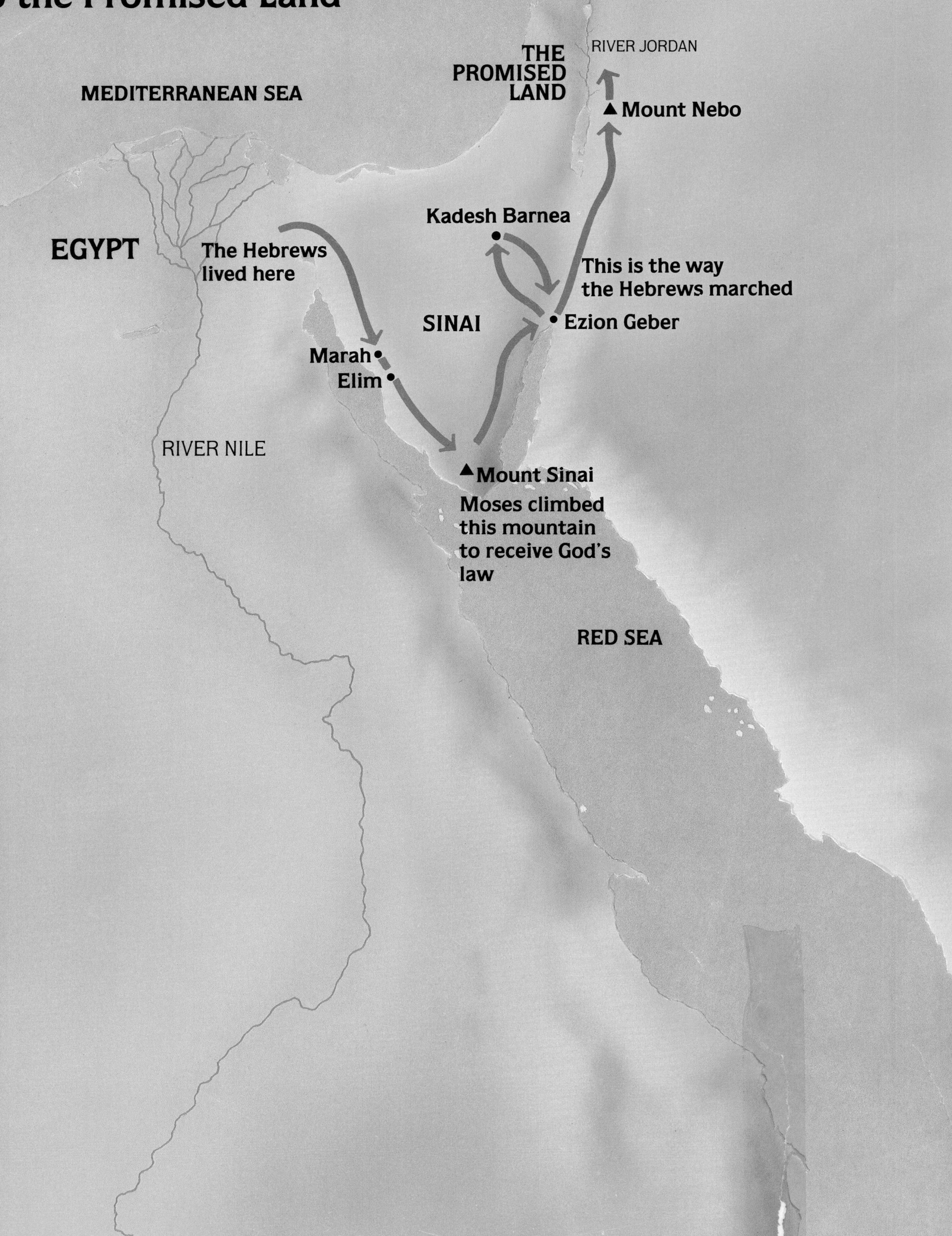